RIKI LEVINSON

OUR HOME
IS THE SEA

PAINTINGS BY DENNIS LUZAK

E. P. DUTTON   NEW YORK

amah   a nurse or maid
congee   thin rice soup
sampan   very small boat
tram   double-deck trolley

LIBRARY OF CONGRESS CATALOGING-IN-PUBLICATION DATA
Levinson, Riki.
   Our home is the sea/by Riki Levinson;
paintings by Dennis Luzak
      p. cm.
   Summary: A Chinese boy hurries home from school to
his family's houseboat in Hong Kong harbor. It is the end of
the school year, and he is anxious to join his father and
grandfather in their family profession, fishing.
   ISBN 0-525-44406-8
   [1. Boat living—Hong Kong—Fiction.   2. Hong Kong—Fiction.]
I. Luzak, Dennis, ill.   II. Title.   87-36419
PZ7.L5796Ou   1988   CIP
[E]—dc19   AC

Published in the United States by E. P. Dutton,
2 Park Avenue, New York, N.Y. 10016,
a division of NAL Penguin Inc.

Published simultaneously in Canada by
Fitzhenry & Whiteside Limited, Toronto

Editor: Ann Durell   Designer: Riki Levinson

Printed in Hong Kong by South China Printing Co.
First Edition   W   10 9 8 7 6 5 4 3 2 1

to my daughter Gerry,
and my friend Lam Tung-ki
R.L.

for Kevin, Tim, and DeWitt,
their summers and their seas
D.L.

Our home is the sea, grandfather said to my father, and father said to me.

I am the eldest son, just like my father. When he was a boy, he did not go to school. I wish I didn't have to. I could be with my father all the time.

Soon he will come for me, for today is my last day of school.

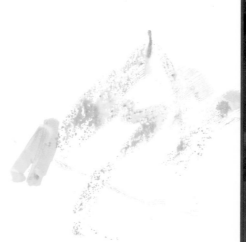

I stuff my report card into a pocket.
I do not want mother to see it. She will
say that I will be a schoolteacher someday.
That is not what I want to be.

I stand on the hill near my school.
I can see the sea. My sea.

Down, down the hill I run, to take
the tram home.

I get on the tram quickly, run up the
stairs, and sit down to watch.
   The tram moves slowly. I cannot wait.

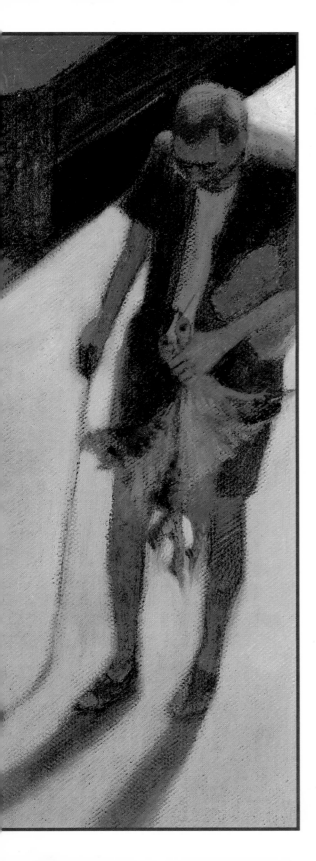

We ride through market streets. People crowd around the carts.

A mother with a baby strapped on her back bends up and down, up and down. The baby sleeps.

A man walks through the street carrying two birds. They make loud noises. I do not think they like to be carried by their necks.

At the end of the street, the tram stops. The light is red.

A school bus crosses to the other side of the road.

Little children hop off the bus. Amahs are waiting to take them home.

I cannot wait for the light to turn green.

The tram turns slowly onto a wide street, past tall houses with windows full of plants and drying clothes. I would not want to live in a tall house.

I watch for the park.

When the tram stops, I hurry down the stairs and get off.

I run into the park.

I see an old man standing straight and still under a gingko tree. Slowly he lifts his arms and sweeps them around, and stands still again. He looks like a bird.

As quietly as I can, I walk past the old man.

I see the birdmen come and hang
their cages on a low berry tree. The men
sit down to talk. I think the birds talk
to each other too.

I see the peacocks. One comes near and stares at me. I stare back. The peacock lifts its head and spreads its feathers wide. I spread my arms. I wish I had feathers like the peacock.

At the end of the park, I run up the
long steps and cross over the harbor road.
I can see our house on the water. I wave.
Middle brother and little brother wave back
as I run down the steps to the wharf.

I put my schoolbag down, take off my shoes, and wait for mother to come. She poles our sampan to the water's edge. I step down into our little boat to go home.

When we get there, I put my schoolbag away. I will not need it for a long time.

Middle brother and little brother and
I sit down on the floor. Mother fills our
bowls with congee and pours the tea.

The night mist falls gently down as
we eat.

I go to bed early. I cannot wait for
tomorrow. My father will come, back
from the sea.

Early in the morning, I hear my mother
and father talking. I get out of bed quickly
and go to him. He puts his hand on my
shoulder. I am glad he is near me.

After we eat, we climb down into
our sampan and ride out, past the jetty,
to grandfather's big boat.

Father and I climb up the ladder.

Mother calls and tells him I will be a
schoolteacher someday.

I look at my father. He looks at me.
We do not say a word.

I will be a fisherman, like my father
and grandfather. Our home is the sea.